IRISH
Activity Book

Lynn Adams

DOVER PUBLICATIONS, INC.
Mineola, New York

NOTE

Enjoy the charms of Ireland while teasing your brain with this delightful little activity book. These fun puzzles and mazes are all illustrated, and include instructions and solutions (the solutions begin on page 53). Solving these puzzles will keep you entertained on trips or after school. You will learn to count and spell, follow the dots, search for hidden words, find differences, and decipher codes. And of course the drawings can be colored in.

Sail across the choppy sea to Ireland.

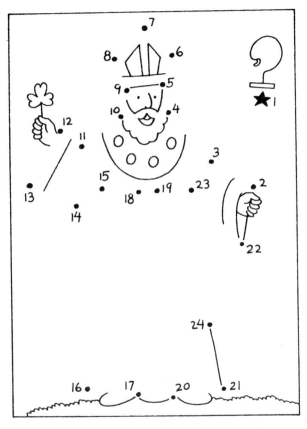

Connect the dots to reveal the Patron Saint of Ireland.

Find the 8 differences in the pictures of Pegeen kissing the Blarney Stone.

7

Find 10 gold coins for the leprechaun.

8

Find the right path to fetch the potatoes.

5	13	5	18	1	12

1	2	3	4	5	6	7	8	9	10	11	12	13
A	B	C	D	E	F	G	H	I	J	K	L	M

Using the key, decipher the code to spell
Ireland's nickname.

4			9	19	12	5

14	15	16	17	18	19	20	21	22	23	24	25	26
N	O	P	Q	R	S	T	U	V	W	X	Y	Z

Find the 11 differences between these two pictures of Sean and his pot of gold.

Using the key, decipher the code to see who drove
the snakes from Ireland.

20	18	9	3	11

14	15	16	17	18	19	20	21	22	23	24	25	26
N	O	P	Q	R	S	T	U	V	W	X	Y	Z

15

Follow the right path to scoop up the shamrocks
and plant them in the pot.

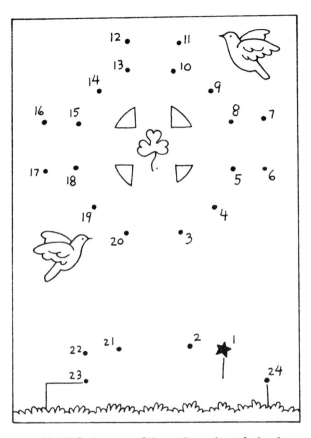

You'll find many of these throughout Ireland.
Connect the dots to see what it is.

Find the eight differences in the two pictures
of St. Patrick.

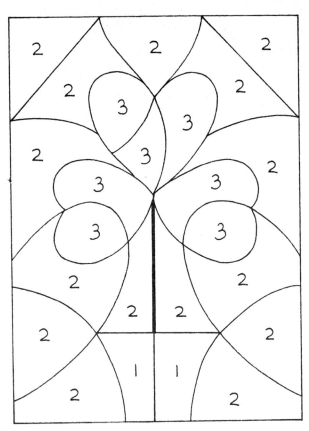

Color the sections marked 1. Red; 2. Yellow; 3. Green and see what appears.

Circle the leprechaun's hat.

The stems of these shamrocks are all tangled up.
Can you follow the stems to find what shamrock
is growing from which pot?

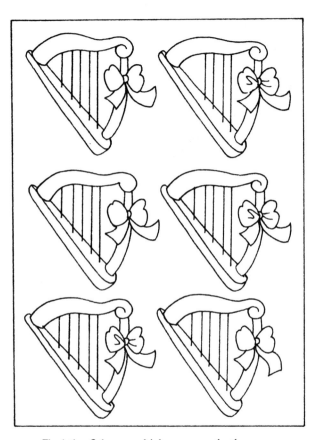

Find the 2 harps which are exactly the same.

12	5	16	18	5

1	2	3	4	5	6	7	8	9	10	11	12	13
A	B	C	D	E	F	G	H	I	J	K	L	M

Using the key, decipher the code to determine
who is hiding here?

3	8	1	21	14

14	15	16	17	18	19	20	21	22	23	24	25	26
N	O	P	Q	R	S	T	U	V	W	X	Y	Z

There are 6 things wrong in this picture of
a leprechaun doing a jig. Can you find them?

Help the leprechaun find the pot of gold.

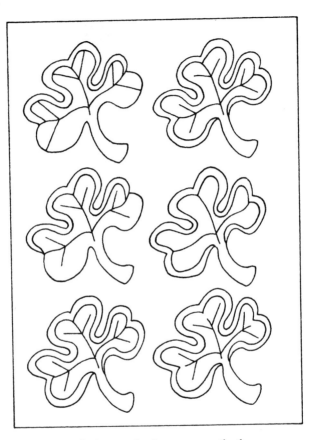

Find the 2 shamrocks that are exactly the same.

Hidden in this picture are a heart, bell, frying pan, crescent moon, candle, and an artist's paintbrush. Can you find them?

Y	L	G	F	C	S	I	R
V	C	U	I	M	L	K	Y
N	O	K	M	E	G	A	N
A	L	G	O	V	E	N	F
K	E	V	I	N	S	E	G
R	E	R	F	A	P	R	M
S	N	M	C	K	V	I	N
Q	U	S	E	L	A	N	O
A	V	E	E	C	G	I	V
E	P	A	T	R	I	C	K
W	T	N	P	S	K	F	L

Find the following Irish names in the search-a-word puzzle: Colleen, Megan, Erin, Patrick, Kevin, Sean. The names can be spelled side-to-side or up-and-down.

There are 8 things wrong in this picture.
Can you find them?

Find the 9 differences between these two pictures of Margaret taking fresh potatoes to her grandmother.

33

G	Y	E	R	F	V	X	S
J	G	R	E	E	N	A	F
E	C	W	S	U	I	G	Q
V	I	R	T	F	Y	O	J
K	R	C	X	P	E	L	G
W	I	S	L	A	N	D	O
T	S	C	K	G	W	L	H
E	H	S	E	R	I	J	A
P	A	K	V	T	B	R	S
H	P	O	T	A	T	O	C
P	J	W	X	Y	Q	V	N

Find the following words in the search-a-word puzzle:
Island, Green, Irish, Potato, Gold. The words can be
spelled side-to-side or up-and-down.

Help Kevin find his Shillelagh and his hat.

Find 2 Shillelaghs that are exactly the same.

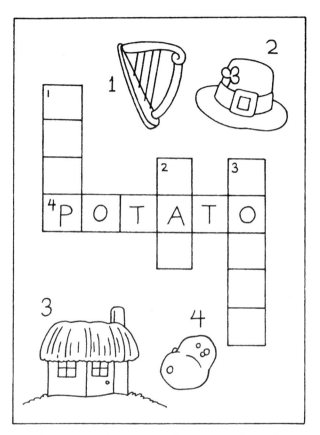

To complete the crossword puzzle, spell out the names of the four pictures. The number next to each picture tells where its name belongs on the grid.

Find Colleen's other shoe to match
the one she's wearing.

E	C	I	G	O	C	A	S
H	I	R	E	L	A	N	D
A	H	A	I	E	S	B	H
S	T	I	R	P	T	O	T
H	T	N	A	I	L	W	C
A	P	B	I	H	E	G	E
T	L	O	R	A	N	I	H
C	A	W	E	R	E	P	I
L	D	I	G	P	H	A	B
T	C	O	T	T	A	G	E
E	S	R	A	N	B	O	W

Find the following words in the search-a-word puzzle:
Castle, Harp, Cottage, Rainbow, Hat, Ireland. The
words can be spelled side-to-side or up-and-down.

Circle the one thing you will find in
the leprechaun's pot.

Find the 13 differences in these pictures of Kevin walking with his lamb.

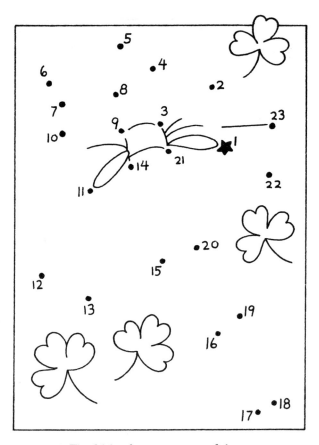

The Irish often carry one of these.
Connect the dots to find out what it is.

Count the potatoes and put them in the
correct basket.

D	U	B	I	N	A	Y	N
U	D	U	B	L	I	N	I
B	I	D	Y	O	Y	C	D
A	B	L	C	I	R	K	U
K	A	C	A	R	U	I	B
E	N	O	K	E	L	L	S
L	T	R	I	D	N	D	U
C	R	U	C	O	R	A	L
B	Y	L	O	L	Y	R	I
A	N	T	R	Y	U	E	N
N	I	Y	K	A	L	L	S

Find the following Irish cities in the search-a-word puzzle: Bantry, Dublin, Cork, Kells, Kildare. The words can be spelled side-to-side or up-and-down.

7 snakes are hiding from St. Patrick.
Can you find them?

3 things belong in an Irish stew. Can you circle them?

Maggie has 2 shamrocks. Find 7 more.

16	15	20		15	6

1	2	3	4	5	6	7	8	9	10	11	12	13
A	B	C	D	E	F	G	H	I	J	K	L	M

Using the key, find out
what is at the end of the rainbow.

7	15	12	4

14	15	16	17	18	19	20	21	22	23	24	25	26
N	O	P	Q	R	S	T	U	V	W	X	Y	Z

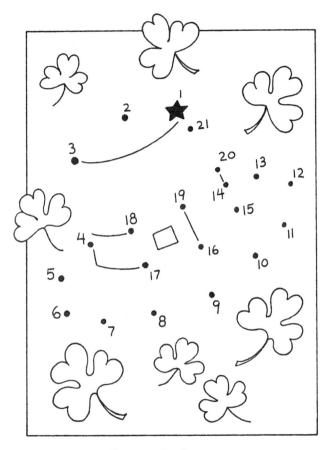

Connect the dots to see
what is hidden in the shamrocks.

Solutions

page 4

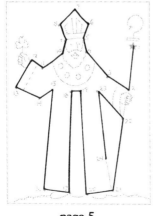

page 5

page 7

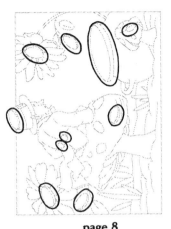

page 8

page 9

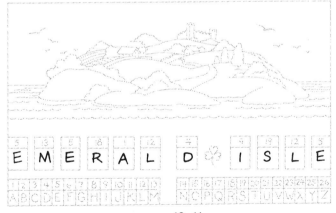

pages 10–11

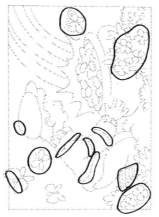

page 13

pages 14–15

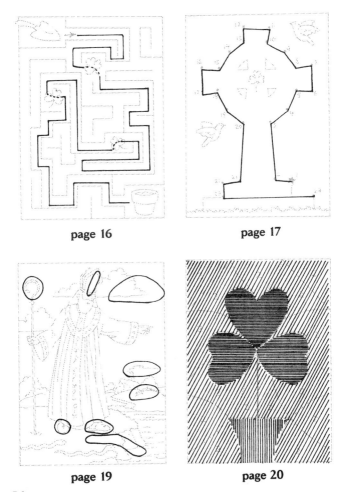

page 16

page 17

page 19

page 20

56

page 21

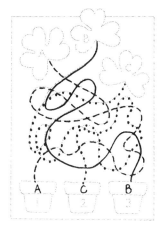

page 22

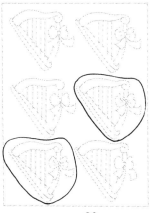

page 23

pages 24–25

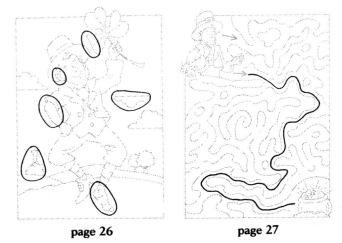

page 26

page 27

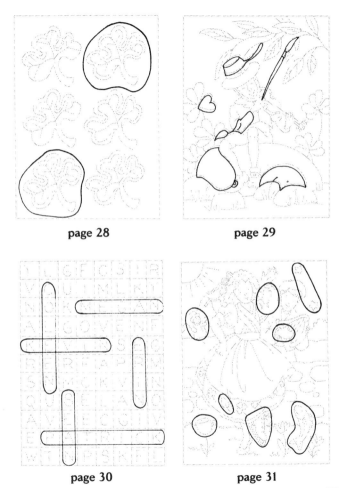

page 28

page 29

page 30

page 31

59

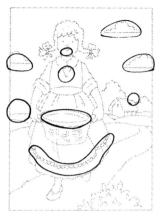

page 33

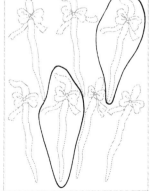

page 34

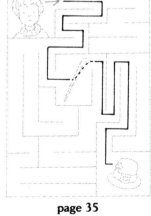

page 35

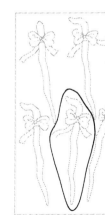

page 36

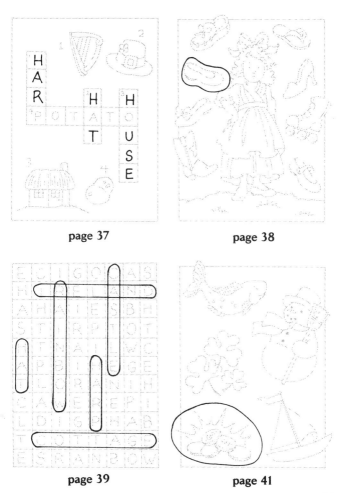

page 37

page 38

page 39

page 41

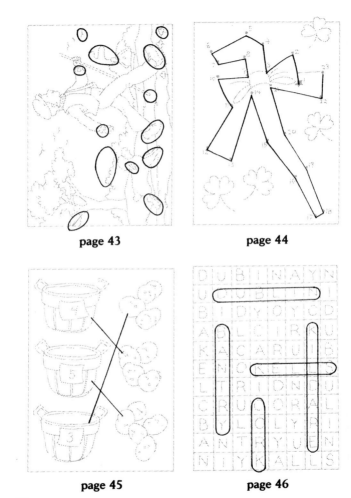

page 43

page 44

page 45

page 46

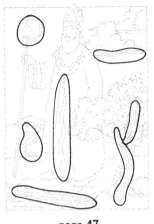

page 47

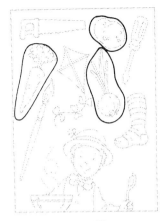

page 48

page 49

P O T O F G O L D

pages 50–51

page 52